The Nutcracker

Illustrated by Anna Luraschi

Retold by Susanna Davidson

It was Christmas Eve.
The world was
covered in a crisp
blanket of snow.

Everything was dazzling white,
except for the golden light
that spilled out from
Clara's house.

Inside, a party was in full swing.
Clara stared out of the window...

She was waiting for something
magical to happen.

Suddenly,
the door burst open.

Merry Christmas, Clara!

It was her godfather.

"I've brought you a
wonderful present,"
he said.

"What can it be?"
wondered Clara, as she
lay in bed that night.

She was so excited,
she couldn't wait
to find out.

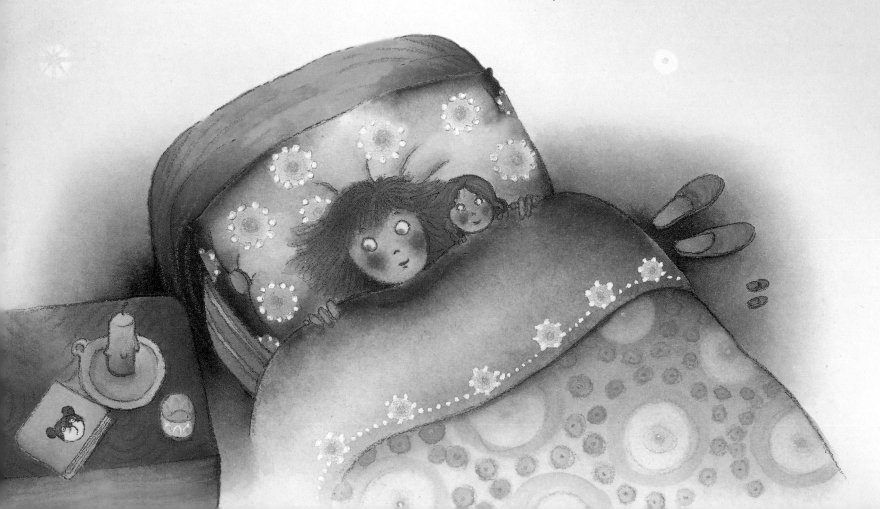

Clara ran downstairs...
and ripped off the
wrapping paper.

Inside was a
nutcracker toy.

Clara hugged him tight.
Then, with a yawn, she
curled up under the tree.
Soon, she was fast asleep.

Dong! Dong! The clock struck midnight. Clara woke with a start. There was a great whooshing sound.

The Christmas tree was rising up above her.

What's happening?

"Hello Clara," whispered a voice behind her.

"My nutcracker?" gasped Clara. He bowed. "I'm the Nutcracker Prince," he said.

"I've come to protect you.
The kitchen mice are plotting
to kidnap you."

He blew sharply on his whistle and six soldiers marched out of the toy box.

They were just in time. The kitchen
mice stormed out of
the shadows.

Ready! Aim! Fire!

The soldiers struck them down with lumps
of cheese and sprayed them with water.

"Is cheese the best you can do?" jeered an evil voice. It was the Mouse King.

He whipped out his sword and lunged at the Nutcracker Prince.

CLANG! CLASH!
went their swords.
"I must help!"
thought Clara.

She took off her slipper
and threw it.

Weeeeeeeeeeeeeeeeee!

It whizzed through the
air and knocked the King out cold.

"You were brilliant!" said the Nutcracker Prince.
"Now we must celebrate."

He called for his reindeer and his magical,
golden sleigh. Clara and the Prince
climbed aboard.

They flew through an open window and into the snow-filled sky.

The reindeer rode through the night.
Far below, Clara could see lollipop trees
and marshmallow flowers.

"Welcome to the Land of Sweets,"

announced the Prince.

They rode up to a marzipan castle,
decorated with all kinds of treats.

"I'm so glad you've come,"
said a dazzling fairy, dancing
out to greet them.

I am the Sugarplum Fairy.
Come inside and eat.

Clara and the Prince
sat down to a feast of
cookies and cakes
and candy swirls.

Then they watched
dances from around
the world.
Spinning Spanish dancers
clicked their castanets.

Arabian princesses
swirled...

...Chinese tea dancers
whirled...

...flower ballerinas twirled.

Clara watched, enchanted.

But the slow, soothing
music called her to sleep.
"It's time to go home,"
whispered the
Nutcracker Prince.

When Clara woke
up, she was under
the Christmas
tree once more
and the Prince
had gone.

"He's only a wooden toy!"
cried Clara. "It must have been
a dream. Unless... unless...
it was the magic of
Christmas Eve."

To Clara,
This present isn't all
that it seems...
From your Godfat

The Nutcracker started life as a story, but in 1892,
a Russian composer named Tchaikovsky turned it
into a ballet. It is now performed all over the world,
especially at Christmas time.

Based on an adaptation by Emma Helbrough
Edited by Jenny Tyler and Lesley Sims

This edition published in 2011. First published in 2006 by Usborne Publishing Ltd, 83-85 Saffron Hill, London EC1N 8RT, England. www.usborne.com
Copyright © 2011, 2006 Usborne Publishing Ltd. The name Usborne and the devices 🎈 🎈 are Trade Marks of Usborne Publishing Ltd. All rights reserved.
No part of this publication may be reproduced, stored in a retrieval system, or transmitted in any form or by any means, electronic, mechanical, photocopying, recording
or otherwise, without the prior permission of the publisher. First published in America in 2011. UE.

As the clock strikes midnight on Christmas Eve, Clara's nutcracker toy turns into a prince. He calls for his reindeer and his golden sleigh and whisks Clara away to the mouth-watering Land of Sweets.

Based on the story behind the famous ballet, this enchanting retelling captures the magic and wonder of Clara's adventure.

CE

£5.99
CAD $9.95

JFMAMJJAS ND/17
01366/06
Printed in China
Made with paper from a sustainable source.

www.usborne.com

ISBN 978-1-4095-3678-9